KT-599-697

the CAVE

Rob Hodgson

Frances Lincoln
Children's Books

There is a cave.

A cave that is home to
a little creature.

A little creature that never
leaves its cave...

... because of a wolf.

'Why don't you come out to play,
little creature?' asks the wolf.

'I'm sure we'd be VERY good friends.'

'No, thank you,' replies the little creature.
'I already have two friends.'

So the little creature stays home.

The wolf comes back day after day.

'Why don't you come out to play,
little creature?' asks the wolf.
'I bet you're SO bored in there,
all cooped up in your cave.'

'No, thank you,' replies the little creature.
'Only boring creatures get bored.'

So the little creature stays home.

The wolf never leaves.

Not even to go to sleep.

But the little creature never comes out.

It doesn't want to climb a tree...

or play ball...

or pick flowers...

and it definitely doesn't want to feed the birds.

'Why don't you come out to play,
little creature?' asks the wolf eventually.

'I'M GETTING HUNGRY NOW!'

'I mean… er… YOU must be
getting hungry n—"

'Aaar^rrgg^hhbzzz^z^zurg^h!'

The little creature sniffs.
'Now you mention it,
I am a *little* hungry.'

'Well,' says the wolf.
'I have the most tasty doughnut
here with YOUR name on it!
Why don't you come and get it?!'

'Does it have sprinkles?'
the little creature asks.

'YES!'
shouts the wolf.

And with a stretch and
a shuffle, the little creature...

COMES OUT
TO PLAY!

'I DO love doughnuts,'
says the bear.

'But I'm still a little hungry…'

'Why don't you come out
to play, little creature?'
asks the bear.

'I'm sure we'd be VERY good friends.'

for little creatures everywhere - R.H.

Brimming with creative inspiration, how-to projects, and useful information to enrich your everyday life, Quarto Knows is a favourite destination for those pursuing their interests and passions. Visit our site and dig deeper with our books into your area of interest: Quarto Creates, Quarto Cooks, Quarto Homes, Quarto Lives, Quarto Drives, Quarto Explores, Quarto Gifts, or Quarto Kids.

Text and illustrations © 2017 Rob Hodgson.

First published in 2017 by Frances Lincoln Children's Books
This paperback edition published in 2019 by Frances Lincoln Children's Books,
an imprint of The Quarto Group.
The Old Brewery, 6 Blundell Street, London N7 9BH, United Kingdom.
T (0)20 7700 6700 F (0)20 7700 8066 www.QuartoKnows.com

The right of Rob Hodgson to be identified as the author and illustrator of this work has been asserted by him in accordance with the Copyright, Designs and Patents Act, 1988 (United Kingdom).

All rights reserved.

No part of this publication may be reproduced, stored in a retrieval system, or transmitted, in any form, or by any means, electrical, mechanical, photocopying, recording or otherwise without the prior written permission of the publisher or a licence permitting restricted copying.

A catalogue record for this book is available from the British Library.

The illustrations were created using mixed and digital media
Set in Baskerville

Published by Rachel Williams
Designed by Andrew Watson
Edited by Katie Cotton
Production by Laura Grandi

Manufactured in Guangdong, China CC 032019

9 8 7 6 5 4 3 2 1